I Want a Hippopotamus for Christmas

I Want a Hippopotamus for Christmas

Words and Music by **John Rox**   Illustrated by **Bruce Whatley**

HARPER

An Imprint of HarperCollinsPublishers

I Want a Hippopotamus for Christmas
Text and music copyright © 1950, 1953 by Folkways Music Publishers, Inc.
© Renewed 1978, 1981 by Edwin H. Morris & Company, A Division of MPL
Communications, Inc.
Illustrations copyright © 2005 by Bruce Whatley

Library of Congress Cataloging-in-Publication Data
Rox, John.
  I want a hippopotamus for Christmas / by John Rox ; illustrated by Bruce Whatley.— 1st ed.
    p.   cm.
  Summary: An illustrated version of the song about a child who wants a
hippopotamus for Christmas.
  ISBN 978-0-06-304321-3
  [1. Children's songs, English—Texts. 2. Hippopotamus—Songs and music.
3. Christmas—Songs and music. 4. Songs.] I. Whatley, Bruce, ill. II. Title.
PZ8.3.R7975Iw 2005   2003011028
[782.42]—dc22   CIP
                                                                       AC

20 21 22 23 24 RTLO 10 9 8 7 6 5 4 3 2 1
❖

I want a hippopotamus for Christmas,

a hippopotamus is all I want.

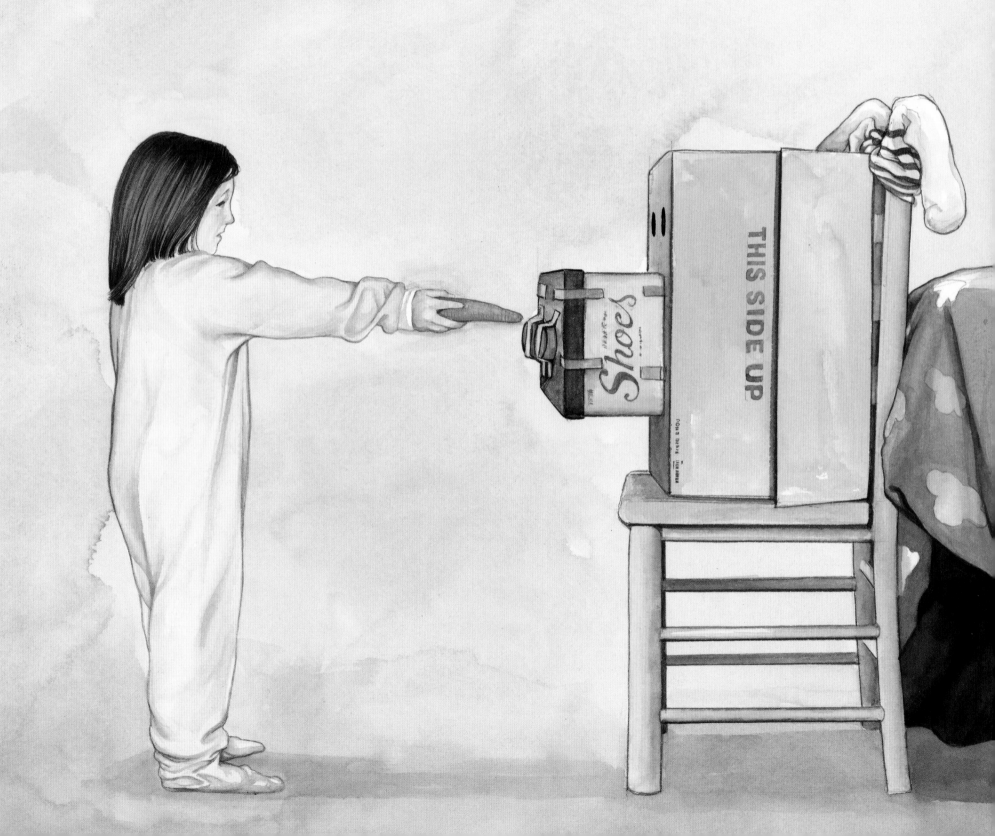

Don't want a doll, no dinky Tinkertoy, I want
a hippopotamus to play with and enjoy.

I want a hippopotamus for Christmas, I don't think
Santa Claus will mind, do you?

He won't have to use our dirty chimney flue, just bring him through the front door, that's the easy thing to do.

I can see me now on Christmas morning, creeping
down the stairs. Oh, what joy and what surprise when
I open up my eyes to see my hippo hero standing there.

I want a hippopotamus for Christmas, only a hippopotamus will do. No crocodiles or rhinoceroses, I only like hippopotamuses and hippopotamuses like me too.

I want a hippopotamus for Christmas,
a hippopotamus is all I want.
Mom says a hippo would eat me up, but then
Teacher says a hippo is a vegetarian.

I want a hippopotamus for Christmas, the kind I saw last summer in the zoo.

We got a car with room for two in our two-car garage, I'd feed him there and wash him there and give him his massage.

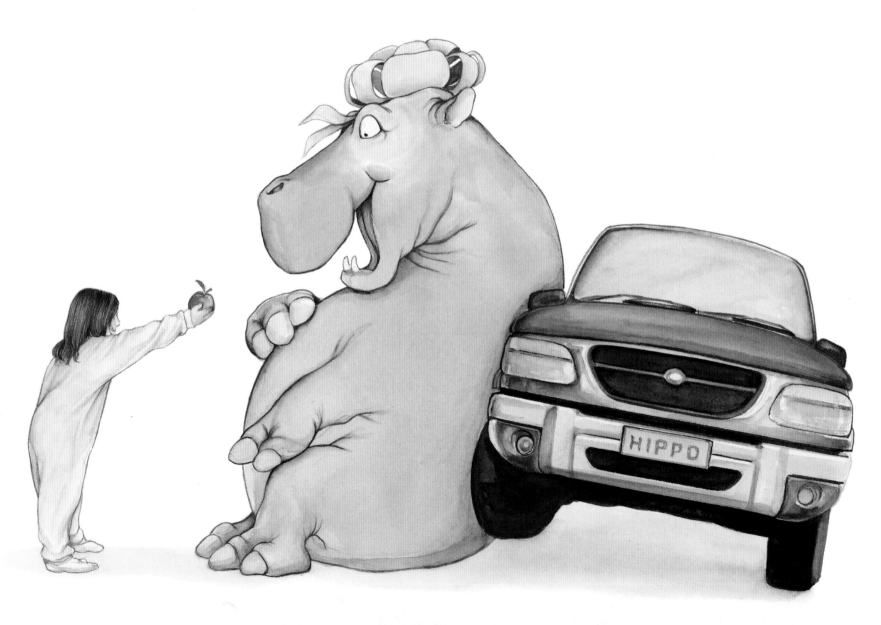

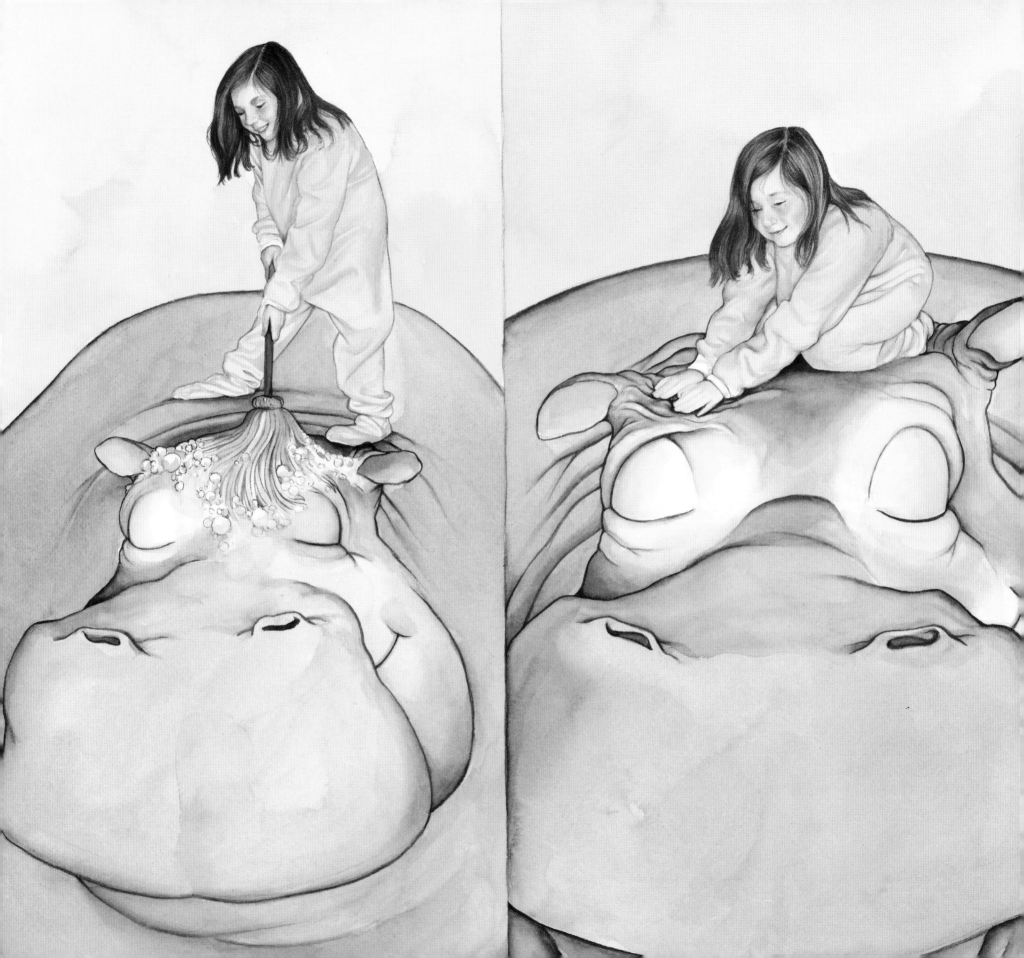

I can see me now on Christmas morning creeping down the stairs. Oh, what joy and what surprise when I open up my eyes

to see my hippo hero standing there.

I want a hippopotamus for Christmas,
only a hippopotamus will do.
No kangaroos or duckbill platypuses,
I only like hippopotamuses

and hippopotamuses like me too.

I Want a Hippopotamus for Christmas

Words and Music by John Rox

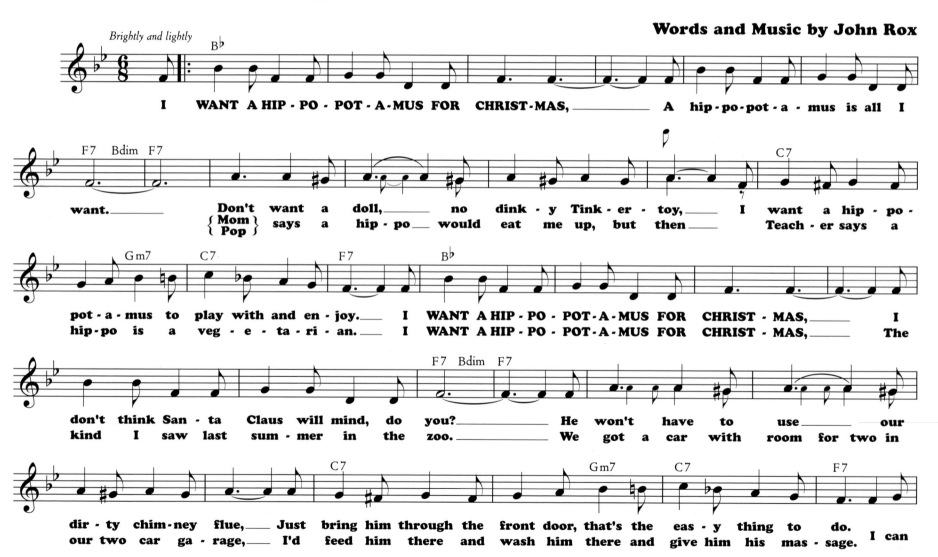

Brightly and lightly

I WANT A HIP - PO - POT - A - MUS FOR CHRIST - MAS, _____ A hip - po - pot - a - mus is all I

want. _____ Don't want a doll, _____ no dink - y Tink - er - toy, _____ I want a hip - po -
{ Mom } says a hip - po _____ would eat me up, but then _____ Teach - er says a
{ Pop }

pot - a - mus to play with and en - joy. _____ I WANT A HIP - PO - POT - A - MUS FOR CHRIST - MAS, _____ I
hip - po is a veg - e - ta - ri - an. _____ I WANT A HIP - PO - POT - A - MUS FOR CHRIST - MAS, _____ The

don't think San - ta Claus will mind, do you? _____ He won't have to use _____ our
kind I saw last sum - mer in the zoo. _____ We got a car with room for two in

dir - ty chim - ney flue, _____ Just bring him through the front door, that's the eas - y thing to do.
our two car ga - rage, _____ I'd feed him there and wash him there and give him his mas - sage. I can